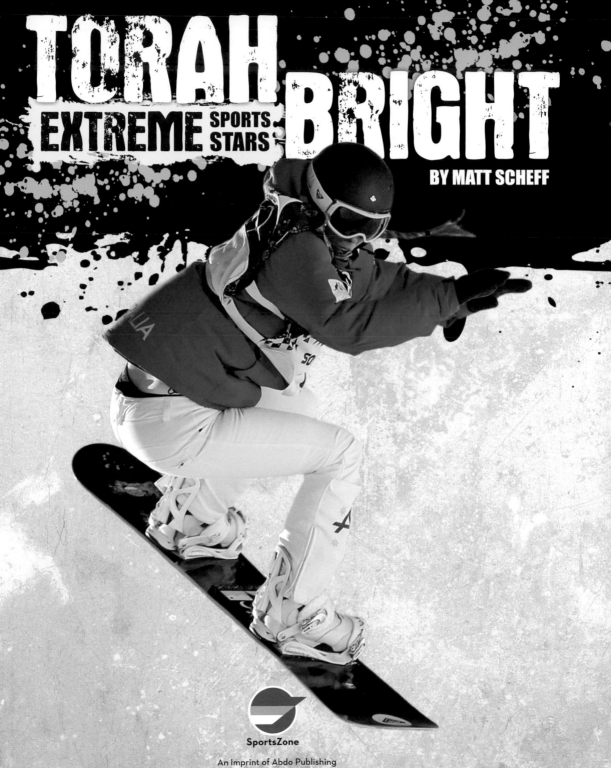

TORAH BRIGHT

EXTREME SPORTS STARS

BY MATT SCHEFF

SportsZone

An Imprint of Abdo Publishing
www.abdopublishing.com

www.abdopublishing.com

Published by Abdo Publishing, a division of ABDO, PO Box 398166,
Minneapolis, Minnesota 55439. Copyright © 2015 by Abdo
Consulting Group, Inc. International copyrights reserved in
all countries. No part of this book may be reproduced in
any form without written permission from the publisher.
SportsZone™ is a trademark and logo of Abdo Publishing.

Printed in the United States of America,
North Mankato, Minnesota
042014
092014

 THIS BOOK CONTAINS
RECYCLED MATERIALS

Cover Photos: Yutaka/AFLO/Icon SMI (foreground);
Andy Wong/AP Images (background)
Interior Photos: Andy Wong/AP Images, 1, 12-13,
14-15, 26 (inset), 28-29, 30 (left); Mark Blinch/
Corbis, 4-5; Marcio Sanchez/AP Images, 6-7, 18;
Franck Faugere/Icon SMI, 8-9; Nathan Bilow/
AP Images, 10-11, 17, 31; Lionel Cironneau/AP
Images, 16, 30 (right); Marc Piscotty/Icon SMI,
19; Erich Schlegel/Icon SMI, 20-21; Chuck Myers/
Icon SMI, 22-23; Felipe Dana/AP Images, 24
(inset), 26-27; Sergei Grits/AP Images, 24-25

Editor: Chrös McDougall
Series Designer: Maggie Villaume

Library of Congress Control Number: 2014933913

Cataloging-in-Publication Data
Scheff, Matt.
 Torah Bright / Matt Scheff.
   p. cm. -- (Extreme sports stars)
Includes index.
ISBN 978-1-62403-457-2
1. Bright, Torah, 1986- --Juvenile literature. 2.
Snowboarders--United States--Biography--Juvenile literature.
I. Title.
796.939092--dc23
[B]
                            2014933913

CONTENTS

GOING FOR GOLD

Snowboarder Torah Bright stood at the top of the halfpipe ramp at the 2010 Olympic Winter Games in Canada. She was in last place in the women's halfpipe finals after a crash in her first run. But in halfpipe, only the best score out of two runs counts. Torah still had a chance.

Torah competes in the halfpipe at the 2010 Olympics.

Torah dropped into the halfpipe. She landed one clean trick after another. The fans went nuts when she stuck a switch backside 720. This dizzying trick features two full rotations in the air and a blind landing. The judges gave Torah a score of 45.0 out of a possible 50. Nobody else could match it. Torah was the gold medalist!

Torah, center, celebrates her 2010 Olympic gold medal in halfpipe snowboarding.

vancouver 2010

FAST FACT

Torah's 2010 gold made her the first Australian snowboarder to win an Olympic medal.

FAST FACT

Torah's brother, Ben, also became a professional snowboarder. Her sister Rowena was an Olympian in downhill skiing.

Torah has always felt at home on the slopes.

LIFE DOWN UNDER

Torah Jane Bright was born on December 27, 1986, in Cooma, Australia. The Bright family loved to ski. Torah was already on skis by age two. Before long, she was an expert at both downhill skiing and cross-country skiing.

Torah competes at the 2008 Winter X Games.

When Torah was around 11 years old, she discovered snowboarding. It didn't take long until she was hooked. She loved doing big jumps and learning new tricks. And she was good at it. She traveled around the world for competitions.

FAST FACT

Torah traveled so much that she couldn't go to a regular school. So she took classes by mail.

BECOMING A STAR

By age 14, Torah had nothing left to prove as an amateur snowboarder. So she decided to turn pro. There was a big problem, though. Australia didn't have much to offer a pro snowboarder. So when she was 15, Torah moved to Salt Lake City, Utah. There, she could train with and compete against the best.

Torah flies through the air during a 2014 practice session.

Torah competes at the 2014 Olympics.

14

By age 16, Torah was really starting to get attention. She had the rare combination of technical skill, big-air ability, and an aggressive approach. Those qualities helped her finish second in the 2003 World Cup. The following year, she won the halfpipe title.

Torah was on the rise. She was named to Australia's 2006 Olympic team. But she finished a disappointing fifth in the halfpipe competition. Torah soon made up for that. She earned a silver medal in the 2006 Winter X Games superpipe event. Then in 2007, she came back to the Winter X Games and claimed the gold.

Torah competes at the 2006 Olympics.

Torah does a trick on the halfpipe at the 2008 Winter X Games.

Torah smiles after winning the 2010 Olympic halfpipe gold medal.

Torah won another Winter X Games gold in superpipe in 2009. But it was at the 2010 Olympic games that she really became a star. Torah was selected to carry the Australian flag at the opening ceremony. That is a great honor for athletes. Then she followed that up with an amazing gold-medal run in the halfpipe event.

Torah flips at the 2008 Winter X Games.

PREPARING FOR SOCHI

Torah was more popular and successful than ever. But it came at a cost. Over the years, she had taken a lot of hard falls. She had suffered several concussions. Torah suffered from bad headaches. So after the 2010 Winter X Games, Torah took a break from competitions. She needed time to heal.

Torah competes in slopestyle at the 2014 Olympics.

Torah had high expectations for the 2014 Olympics.

Torah didn't enter any competitions for approximately two years. But she was still very busy. She married fellow snowboarder Jake Welch in 2010. However, they divorced in 2013. That was hard on Torah. But she continued to practice her snowboarding. She was preparing for the 2014 Olympics in Sochi, Russia, and she had big plans.

Torah smiles after winning the 2014 Olympic silver medal in halfpipe.

Torah lands a halfpipe trick at the 2014 Olympics.

In 2014, Torah made history. For the first time, the Olympics had five snowboarding events. Torah qualified in halfpipe, slopestyle, and snowboard cross. She became the first snowboarder to qualify in three events. Torah didn't have much success in boardercross. But she took seventh in slopestyle and won the silver medal in halfpipe.

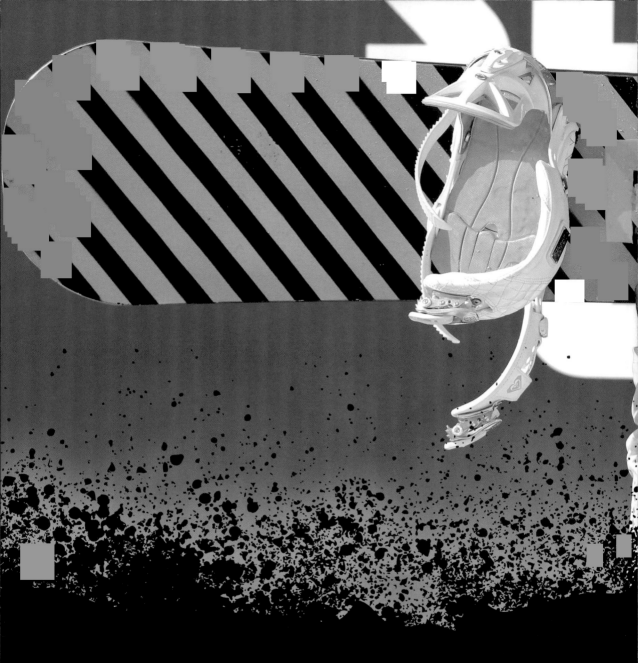

Torah shined at the 2014 Winter Olympics at age 27. But snowboarding is a young person's sport. Will Torah still have what it takes to win a third straight halfpipe medal in the 2018 Winter Games? Her fans can't wait to find out.

Torah hopes to keep dazzling fans with her big tricks for years to come.

СОЧИ

TIMELINE

1986
Torah Jane Bright is born on December 27 in Cooma, Australia.

1989
At age two, Torah begins to ski.

1998
Torah first begins to snowboard at age 11.

2004
Torah wins the World Cup halfpipe title at age 17.

2006
Torah takes the silver medal in the superpipe event at the Winter X Games.

2007
Torah becomes the first Australian snowboarder to win gold at the Winter X Games.

2010
Torah wins the Olympic gold medal in halfpipe. Later that year, she begins a two-year break from competitions.

2014
Torah makes history by qualifying for three different snowboarding events in the same Olympic Games. She takes the silver medal in halfpipe.

GLOSSARY

aggressive
Forceful and intense.

amateur
A person who is not paid to compete in a sport.

concussions
Brain injuries that occur when somebody suffers a jolt to the head.

halfpipe
A type of ramp used in snowboarding and skateboarding, shaped like the letter U.

pro
Short for professional; a person who is paid to compete in a sport.

slopestyle
A snowboarding event in which riders do tricks on a mountain path or "terrain park."

snowboard cross
A competition in which snowboarders race on a downhill course. It is also known as a boardercross.

superpipe
A type of snowboarding halfpipe that is wider than normal halfpipes, with high, vertical walls on both sides.

INDEX